Clarence The Clown

and his

Not-So-Special Day

by Orlando Hobechi and Jim Figueroa
illustrated by Jim Figueroa

HEARTH
&
FireLight
PRESS

Hearth & Firelight Press

Graphic Design – Trefoni Michael Rizzi (TdB Press, LLC)
Clean-up Artist – Kim Bowen

Library of Congress Catalog Card Number: 2008940262

ISBN-13: 978-1-6072539-4-5

This book was printed with vegetable-based inks.
Book boards are 100% recycled, with a minimum of 35% post consumer waste.

Printed in the U.S.A.

Visit us on the web at www.hearthandfirelight.com

HEARTH
&
FireLighT
PRESS

Dedication and Thanks

From Jim:
I dedicate this book to Beth and AJ Figueroa...
because without you two? My life would be... well, not-so-special.
To Tina and the Choices we make.
And to Orlando Hobechi – to fulfill promise #1.
Special thanks to: The Bowen Clan; the Figueroa Gang;
the Martin Tribe; my WFM Family; Tony & Tedrick;
and to my true friends who inspire me to follow my dreams.

From Orlando:
I would like to offer a VERY SPECIAL thanks to all those
who let me know, (in one way or another)
that I would never accomplish this... or much of anything else.
And this book is sincerely dedicated to those in my life
who never stopped believing that I would (like you, mom).

In a not-so-special town,
in a not-so-special neighborhood,
at the end of a not-so-special street,
there is a house.
Not just any old house,
but my house.

Yes,

it is my house
I am sorry to say.

That is the front door...
not really
a big laughing mouth.

There is the porch light...
not a big, glowing red nose.

Those funny glasses?
They are the window frames.

The Clown hat is our chimney.

And look!

The trees in my back yard look like a silly hairdo.

you might think it is fun to live in a house that looks like a humongous laughing clown's head...

but people always drive by and point and laugh. And do you think my parents mind?

NOPE!

That is them out there on the front lawn making balloon animals for the people driving by: Clyde and Clara T. Clown. My little sister Cloie is the one riding the unicycle and juggling. And that is our dog Clumpy bouncing on that ball. Right now I am supposed to be running around with a camera that squirts disappearing ink.

But it is not fun for me.

Just once I'd like to know what it is like to be...
well, not so special.

Just once I'd like to sit down to dinner
and NOT have one of those inflatable cushions
make that *fffththfsphthffshphthppt* noise.

I'd like to get dropped off at school in a normal car.

Not the mini clown car with all of Dad's work buddies!

I wish I could come home to a mom who looks the same each day!

Oh, don't worry, I know it is her.

But sometimes she is tubby.

Sometimes she is very, very tall.

Sometimes she is skinny.

Sometimes she is short.

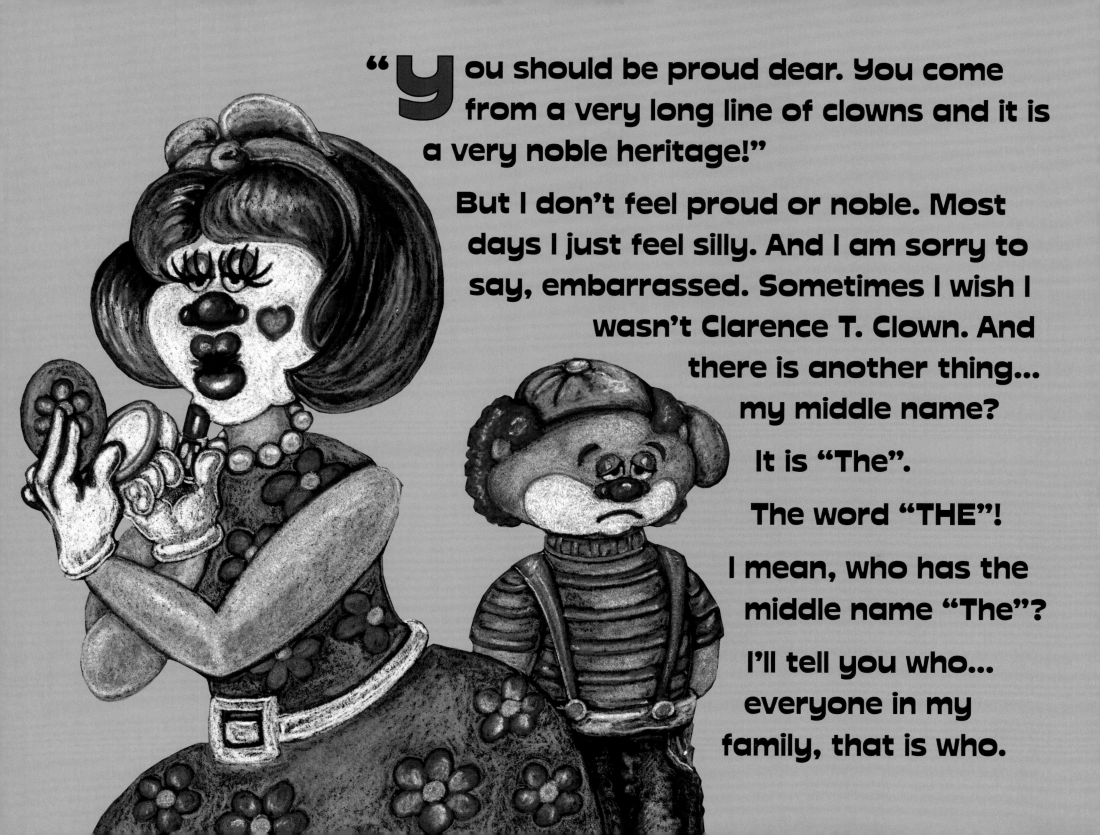

"**Y**ou should be proud dear. You come from a very long line of clowns and it is a very noble heritage!"

But I don't feel proud or noble. Most days I just feel silly. And I am sorry to say, embarrassed. Sometimes I wish I wasn't Clarence T. Clown. And there is another thing... my middle name?

It is "The".

The word "THE"!

I mean, who has the middle name "The"?

I'll tell you who... everyone in my family, that is who.

Clyde The...   Clara The...   Cloie The...
Even my dog – Clumpy The...
And of course me – Clarence The...   Clown.

Mom and Dad figured out I have been miserable lately.

It was just last week they caught me watching Educational Television. I tried to change the channel to cartoons real quick, but I know they saw me.

And it was just last week that mom came across my hidden copies of News Month Magazine and the Wallet Street Journal.

That is why after entertaining the neighbors tonight we are supposed to have a "Family Meeting".

I will have to sit and listen to another talk about the Clown Family name, making people laugh, and not disappointing them.

"**Son, your mother and I have noticed you have been unhappy."**

"Yes, you haven't been laughing much lately dear. And you haven't once worn the spinning bow-tie Uncle Claude and Auntie Claudia got you for your birthday."

"And it has been a long time since you played a joke on the mailman. Clarence, do you know what we want most for you?"

Yes Dad. To be a Clown, to make people laugh, and to live up to the Clown family heritage. I know.

"Well I know it seems that way Son, but more than anything, your mom and I want you to be happy. So... we have spoke to the Smiths next door and you can spend the whole weekend with them to see what the not-so-special life is all about."

Really? I can be not-so-special for the whole weekend?

WOW! Thanks Mom and Dad!

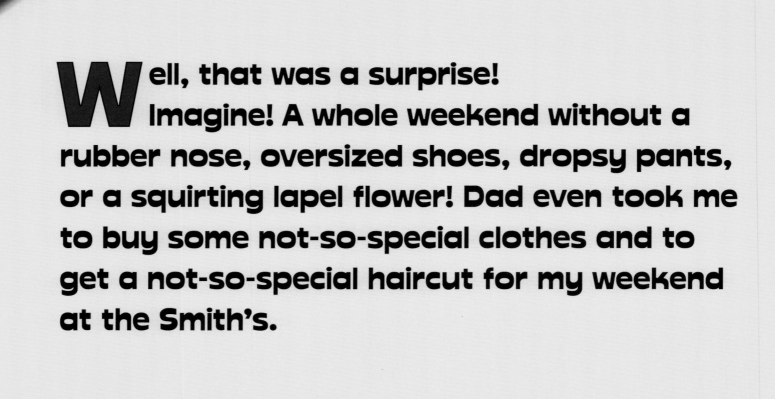

Well, that was a surprise!
Imagine! A whole weekend without a
rubber nose, oversized shoes, dropsy pants,
or a squirting lapel flower! Dad even took me
to buy some not-so-special clothes and to
get a not-so-special haircut for my weekend
at the Smith's.

"**Y**ou look so ordinary Dear! Are you sure this is what you want?"

Yes Mom and Dad, I am sure!

"**W**ell Dear, if you are sure...
    then I guess we are sure.

B-b-b-bye Son! (gulp)
    Wa-a-hh, o-oh,
wa-aa-a-ahhh!!"

Mom, Dad, calm down. I am just next door!

And here we go!

"Clarence, welcome to our home. John Jr., help Clarence get his things to your room and then both of you get washed up and come to dinner."

"Okay mom. Hey Clarence, Mom fixed her specialty tonight: Meat loaf, instant potatoes and canned peas!"

That sounds great! Thanks John Jr.!

This is FANTASTIC! Sitting down to dinner of not-so-special food with my not-so-special neighbors and friends the Smiths!

Dinner conversation tonight was VERY interesting!

"This is some weather we are having eh, dear?"

"Yes it sure is – some weather!"

"And how about that game tonight Son? Some game, eh?"

"Yup! Some game Dad!"

"Boy I'll say! Dear, this sure is some dinner!"

"Yup Mom, it sure is!"

"Well thank you everyone!"

Saturday at the mall! And do you know what we did? You guessed it! Nothing special.

Again we talked about the weather, the game last night, and the food. Oh! And the time! Now that was REALLY interesting!

You know...

Mr. Smith would say, "Well, would you look at the time!"

Then Mrs. Smith would reply, "Gee, would you look at that! Who would have thought!"

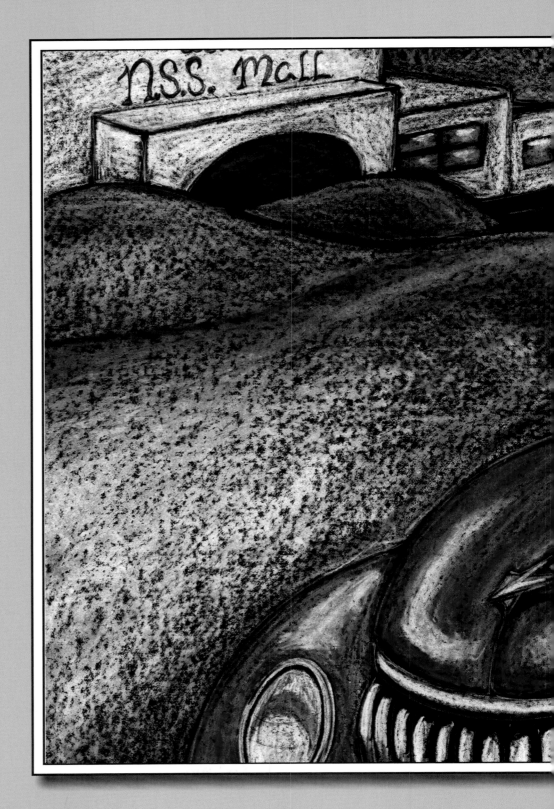

"That is great stuff Mr. and Mrs. S!" I'd say. But they would just look at me strangely and then smile and nod.

Dinner tonight was ummm, leftovers. Then after dinner, we watched TV and John Jr. and I played video games.

"**T**ime for bed boys!"

Okay Mrs. S! Hey Mrs. S. – Night night, sleep tight and don't let the frost bite!
Good night Mrs. S.!

"Oh gosh. Good night boys!"

"Clarence, you and your family sure have a different way of talking. You guys are great! I wish I had a family like yours."

What?! Are you Crazy? Most of the time I wish I wasn't Clarence T. Clown!

"You're kidding me, right? Think of all the fun you must have! And your parents are super! Think of all the people they help."

Excuse me?! My parents "help"?

Why, they just help embarrass me!

"Clarence, don't you remember when my dog 'Spot' died? My dad took me to over to your house. I didn't want to go at first... because I was so sad. But when we got there, your dad took my hand and together we made a balloon animal dog. He even made it look like my dog... with a little paper dog tag around his neck that said 'Spot' on it. But instead of just filling him up with air, your dad filled him up with helium. Then we went to the front yard and your dad said,

'Now, let him go John Jr.' I didn't want to... but your dad said we could make another one if I wanted.

So I let the balloon 'Spot' go.

We watched him float up and up into the sky. I couldn't help but cry. And you know? When I looked at your dad, he was crying too. Then he said, 'When your dog died, John Jr., that part of him that knew you loved him and he was your best friend, floated to heaven. But instead of floating out of sight... he stays where he can see you to make sure you are safe and happy.'

I didn't ask your dad to make me

And sometimes, when I think of 'Spot', I imagine him to be watching me from just above the trees... and I'll say, 'I am fine Boy, but I sure miss you'."

Wow. What could I say? My dad did a really great thing for John Jr. by helping him get through missing his dog.

And as I think about it, Mom and Dad are really pretty cool. They have weird and wonderful ways of teaching me and Cloie stuff and letting us know they love us. They do have a different way of looking at things and a different way of living... but I guess that is what makes them so... special.

"Mom! Dad! Clarence is home!"

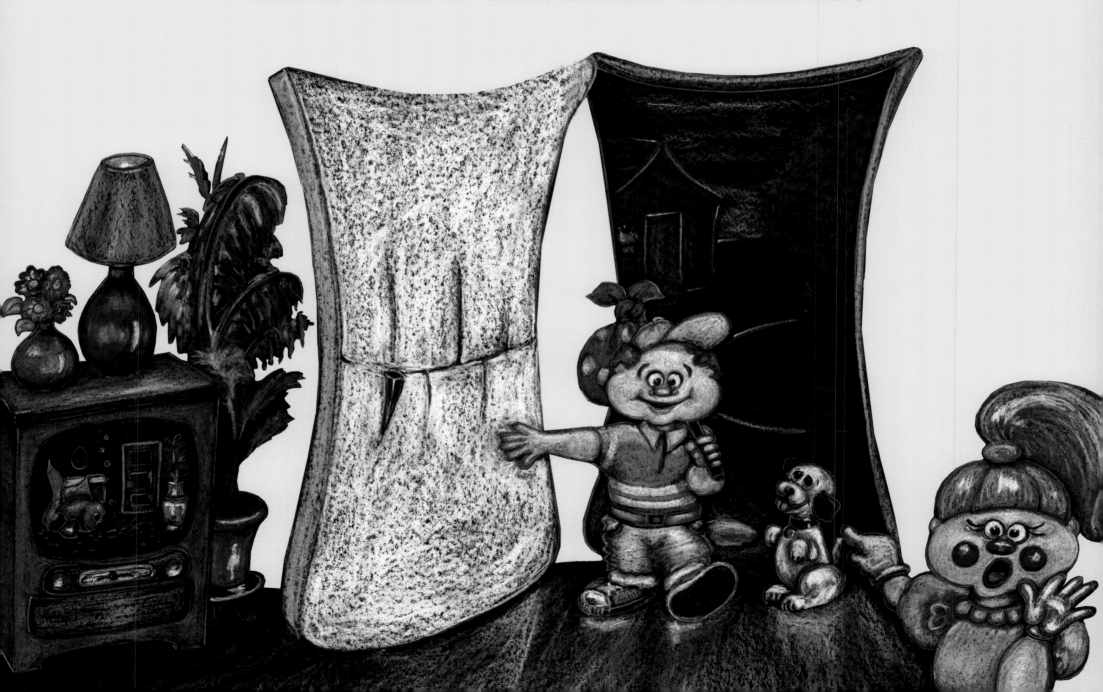

"**H**owdy doo there Son!"
"**Y**es, welcome back to your old stompin' grounds dear!"

"**W**ell m'boy, tell us, where did y'go, what did y'do?"

"**O**h yes honey! And tell me, is Mrs. Smith as good a cook as I am?"

Well Mom, I'd say Mrs. Smith is a pretty good cook. Her specialty is meat loaf, instant potatoes and canned peas.

"**W**ell that sounds nice."

Yeah, it was. We had it for dinner on Friday, dinner on Saturday, and for dinner on Sunday. We had it in sandwiches for lunch and with eggs for breakfast.

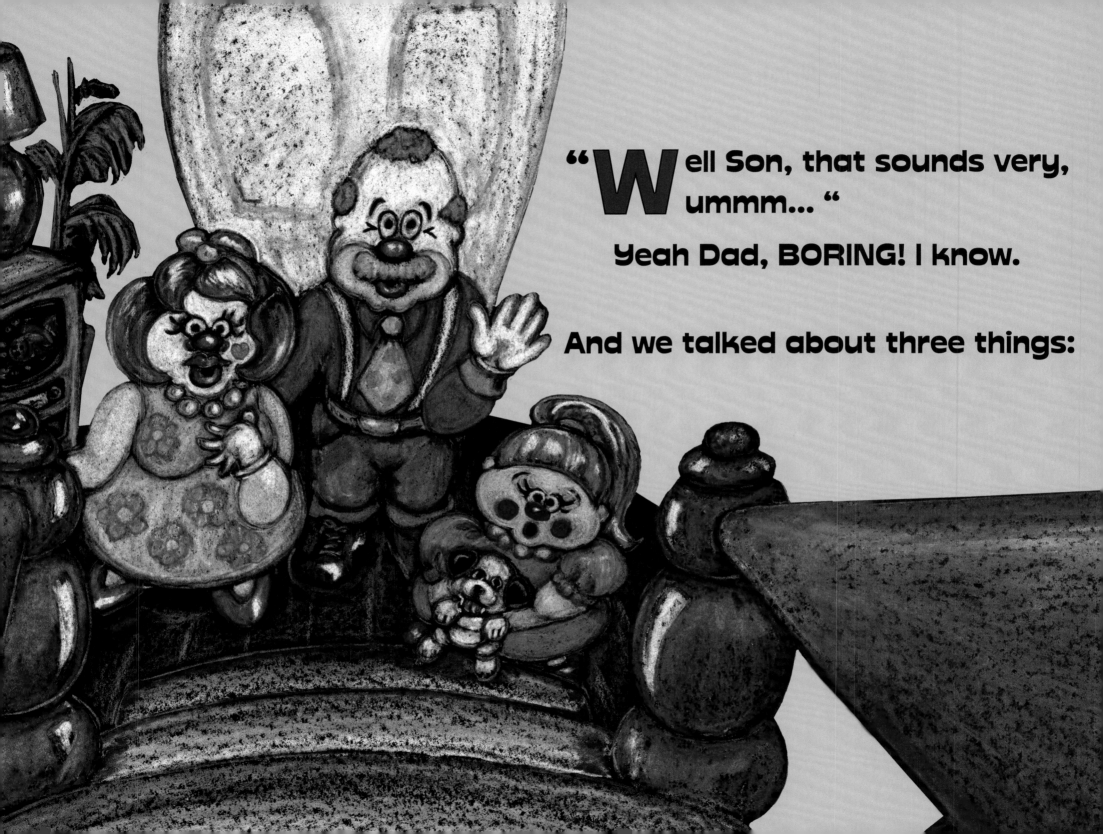

"**W**ell Son, that sounds very, ummm... "

Yeah Dad, BORING! I know.

And we talked about three things:

"This is SOME weather we are having eh?", or "This is SOME dinner, eh?" and "That was SOME game, eh?"

Oh, and I almost forgot! "Well would you look at the time!", and then, "Gee would you look at that! Who would have thought?".

"Who would have thought what Son?"

I don't know Dad, they never said!

"Oh my! Poor John and Mary! I had no idea that is how they lived!"

But you know what Mom? They seem happy. And that is what I like about the Smiths.

"Are you saying you want to be like them Son?

Well Dad, let me put it this way:

After dinner tonight, instead of just watching TV, I did a magic show for them.

"Wow Clarence! Where did you learn to do that?", they all asked.

"I learned it from my DAD", I told them proudly.

hen instead of the regular one scoop of vanilla ice cream for dessert, I baked a batch of Mom's special circus animal cookies, and served them up with her "Rockin Choco Milk".

"These are terrific Clarence!", they all said, "You must have a great chef in your family!"

"Great Chef?" I said, "Nah, me and my mom fix these on special occasions and when she wants people to feel better".

So the not-so-special life may be nice and peaceful, and I do like that sort of thing... but being Clarence T. Clown is a lot of fun and I am proud to have the Clown family name!

"**W**ell your father and I have learned some things ourselves. Haven't we Honey?"

"**Y**our mother is right. Your happiness means more to us than anything. So you can keep that haircut, and wear those not-so-special clothes to school if you'd like. Just keep being a good, kind person, and we'll be proud of you!"

Well how could I be anything else? I have you two for parents!

"**A**www, Son! Now go put your things away before we all start crying."

So, there you have it. My not-so-special day taught me some things I did not expect. And I guess my parents learned some things too!

Gee, would you look at that! Who would have thought? – as the Smiths say.

Hey Clarence!
Come downstairs.
There is one more thing
to talk about.

Hmmm. I wonder what that could be about.

"**S**ee? Your mom fixed your favorite dessert for your homecoming: Cotton Candy Cherry Chip Pie with Fruity poo punch. So sit down and join us!"

fffththfsphthffshphthppt

Oh ... Dad!

About Hearth and Firelight Press

We at Hearth and Firelight Press are committed to sponsoring Children's Literature which is not only entertaining, but is also filled with positive messages for young people.
We are also committed to responsible stewardship of our environment and our communities.
And most of all we want Kids to have fun reading and learning!

The authors of
Clarence The Clown and His Not-So-Special Day
have selected 2 organizations to benefit from the proceeds of each book sale.
One of the authors has faced the challenges and struggles of life
with a severe learning disorder.
For this reason they are endeavoring to support foundations which fund research and create awareness concerning all types of Challenged Learning and Literacy.
For more information about the organizations benefiting from this edition,
visit our website at www.hearthandfirelight.com